To my wife, Judy, and my sons,
Morgan and Matthew—M.P.

To Auntie Barb True—T.K.

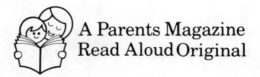

A Parents Magazine
Read Aloud Original

Text Copyright © 1981 by Michael Pellowski
Illustrations Copyright © 1981 by True Kelley
All rights reserved. Printed in the United States of America.
10   9   8   7   6   5   4

Library of Congress Cataloging in Publication Data
Pellowski, Michael.   Clara joins the circus.
SUMMARY: Clara Cow, in search of excitement, tries
to join the circus but seems hopelessly unsuitable
for almost every job.
1. Circus stories.   2. Cows—Fiction
I. Kelley, True.   II. Title
PZ7.P3656C1   E   80-25602
ISBN 0 – 8193 – 1057 – 3   ISBN 0 – 8193 – 1058 – 1 lib. bdg.

CLARA
JOINS THE
CIRCUS

by Michael Pellowski
pictures by True Kelley

Parents Magazine Press / New York

Clara Cow was bored.
Every day she got up at dawn.
She nibbled grass all day.
She went to bed at sunset.
Nothing exciting ever happened.

One afternoon, Clara heard strange noises.
She went up the hill to have a look.

From the hilltop, Clara saw a circus parade.
The Ringmaster, who was leading the parade,
shouted, "Halt!"
The parade stopped.
"We'll camp here," said the Ringmaster.

"Circus life must be exciting,"
said Clara to herself.
"I wonder if I could join."
So she walked down the hill into the circus camp.
She came face to face with the Ringmaster.

Clara smiled. "My name is Clara.
I'd like to join the circus."
The Ringmaster said,
"We're always looking for new acts.
What can you do?"

Clara gulped. "I've never worked
in a circus," she said.
"I don't know WHAT I can do."

"Don't give up," the Ringmaster told her.
"You'll have a chance to try out."

"I'll try my best," Clara promised.
"I want to join the circus
more than anything."

"Good," said the Ringmaster.
"Let's start with tightrope walking."

Clara climbed the ladder.
She stepped out on
the thin, tight line.
"Oh-oh," Clara said.
She began to wobble.
The rope began to wobble.
"Whoops!" cried Clara. "Help!"

Ker-splash!
Clara tumbled off the tightrope
right into a tub of water.
"Well, so much for tightrope walking,"
Clara said. "What's next?"

"Juggling," said the Ringmaster.
Clara picked up three heavy wooden pins.
She tossed them into the air
and tried to juggle.

Bonk! Bonk! Bonk!
One by one the pins landed
on Clara's head.
"Ouch! Ouch! Ouch!" she moaned.
"I guess I can't juggle either.
Maybe I'm a trapeze artist."

Soon Clara was high
above the center ring,
hanging from a trapeze.
"Here I go!" she yelled.

But Clara wasn't a trapeze artist.
Nibbling grass all day had
made her too heavy.
The ropes snapped.
Down came the trapeze.
Down came Clara Cow—
into the safety net.

"Now what?" asked the Ringmaster.
Clara thought a minute.
"I'll be the first cow to be shot
out of a cannon," she said.
The Ringmaster shook his head
as Clara climbed into the cannon.

Halfway in, Clara got stuck.
"Get me out of here!" she hollered.
A great big elephant came to Clara's rescue.
She wrapped her trunk around Clara
and pulled and pulled and pulled.

Finally, out popped Clara.
"Why don't you help me set up tents?"
the elephant suggested.
"I'll try," said Clara.
So off they went.

But when Clara aimed to hit a peg,
she hit her foot instead.
"YEOW!" she bellowed.
"No," said the Ringmaster.
"She can't set up tents either."

"Please," begged Clara.
"Give me another chance."
"There aren't many jobs left,"
said the Ringmaster.
"Do you want to be a lion tamer?"
"No, thank you!"
Clara quickly answered.

"I can't think of anything else,"
said the Ringmaster.
"She could sell peanuts and popcorn
to the crowd," the elephant suggested.
"I know I could do that!" cried Clara.
"Well, all right," agreed the Ringmaster.

Clara went into the main tent.
The Ringmaster gave her a uniform
to wear and a tray filled with bags
of peanuts and popcorn.
"Walk across the tent and
into the stands," he told her.
"Let me hear you yell,
'Peanuts and popcorn!'"

Eagerly Clara walked toward the stands.
She did not look where she was going.
Just as she passed the doorway,
the clowns came rushing in.
Clara didn't see the clowns.
"Oh, no!" cried the Ringmaster.

Bump! Smash! Crash!
Clara went flying this way.
Clowns went flying that way.
Peanuts and popcorn went flying
every which way.
Luckily no one was hurt.

Suddenly, the Ringmaster began to laugh.
Soon everyone in the tent was laughing.
"What a great entrance,"
said the Ringmaster.

"We'll make that accident the opening
of the clown act," said the Ringmaster.
"It will be terrific. Will you do it?"

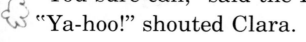

"You mean I can join the circus?" said Clara.
"You sure can," said the Ringmaster.
"Ya-hoo!" shouted Clara.

And that is how Clara Cow
joined the circus.

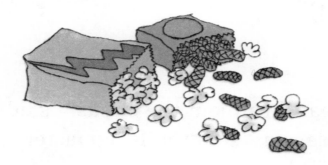

ABOUT THE AUTHOR

MICHAEL PELLOWSKI was a professional football player and then a high school teacher before he turned to writing in 1974. Since then he has written more than fifteeen books for children.

"Writing children's books is my favorite thing to do," says Mr. Pellowski. He always tests his stories on his sons. "If they laugh, then I know other children will laugh too," he says. "And to me, that's what writing is all about."

Mr. Pellowski lives with his wife and two sons in New Jersey.

ABOUT THE ARTIST

TRUE KELLEY has lived almost all her life in New Hampshire. She and her husband are now building a "passive" solar home there. It will use sunshine and wood-burning stoves instead of other energy for fuel.

Ms. Kelley liked Clara immediately because both her mother and grandmother are named Clara. She especially enjoyed illustrating this book because "it has lots of action, color, and foolishness!" She says you have to be careful, though, when you draw a funny picture. "If you laugh," Ms. Kelley explains, "it makes a squiggly line and messes up the picture!"

Ms. Kelley has illustrated several picture books for children, one of which she also wrote.

PARENTS MAGAZINE PRESS *is pleased to welcome both Michael Pellowski and True Kelley to its group of authors and artists.*